Hazel Emerson Hall

Great Books Great Kids

Charlotte Hobbs Library
Lovell, Maine

Hazel – John

Be kind. Even a telephone call that may take your time from something you want to do can help someone else keep their sanity.

Hazel Emerson Hall

MY FIRST LITTLE HOUSE BOOKS

SUGAR SNOW

ADAPTED FROM THE LITTLE HOUSE BOOKS

By Laura Ingalls Wilder

Illustrated by Doris Ettlinger

HARPERCOLLINS PUBLISHERS

To my aunt, Betty Richards

—D.E.

Sugar Snow Text adapted from Little House in the Big Woods, *text copyright 1932, copyright renewed 1959, Roger Lea MacBride. Illustrations copyright © 1998 by Renée Graef. Art direction by Renée Graef. Printed in Hong Kong. All rights reserved. Library of Congress Cataloging-in-Publication Data Wilder, Laura Ingalls, 1867–1957. Sugar snow / adapted from the Little house books by Laura Ingalls Wilder ; illustrated by Doris Ettlinger. p. cm. — (My first little house books) Summary: A cold snap late in winter allows a pioneer girl and her family to enjoy the rich sugar candy made from maple tree sap. ISBN 0-06-025932-9. — ISBN 0-06-025933-7 (lib. bdg.) 1. Wilder, Laura Ingalls, 1867–1957—Juvenile fiction. [1. Wilder, Laura Ingalls, 1867–1957—Fiction. 2. Maple sugar—Fiction. 3. Frontier and pioneer life—Fiction.] I. Wilder, Laura Ingalls, 1867–1957. Little house in the Big Woods. II. Ettlinger, Doris, ill. III. Series. PZ7.S9438 1998 E—DC21 97-14528 CIP AC 2 3 4 5 6 7 8 9 10 ❖*

HarperCollins®, 📖®, and Little House® are trademarks of HarperCollins Publishers Inc.

http://www.harperchildrens.com

Illustrations for the My First Little House Books are
inspired by the work of Garth Williams with his
permission, which we gratefully acknowledge.

Once upon a time, a little girl named Laura lived in the Big Woods of Wisconsin in a little house made of logs.

Laura lived in the little house with her Pa, her Ma, her big sister Mary, her baby sister Carrie, and their good old bulldog Jack.

Spring was coming to the Big Woods. For days the sun shone and the weather was warm. All day the icicles fell one by one from the little house into the snowbanks.

Then one day Laura saw a patch of ground showing through the snow. "May I go out to play, Ma?" she asked.

"You may tomorrow," Ma promised.

That night Laura woke up shivering. Her nose was icy cold. Ma tucked another quilt around her. "Snuggle close to Mary," Ma said, "and you'll get warm."

In the morning Laura looked out the window, and the ground was covered with soft, thick snow. Pa came in, stamping the soft snow from his boots. "It's a sugar snow," he said.

Laura quickly tasted a snowflake from Pa's sleeve, but it didn't taste like sugar at all. "Why is it a sugar snow, Pa?" she asked. Pa said he would explain tonight after he came home from Grandpa's.

It was late when Pa came home that night. He came in with a big bucket and two little packages. He gave the bucket to Ma, and the little packages to Laura and Mary.

The bucket was full of dark brown maple syrup. When Laura opened her little package, she found a little, hard, brown cake with beautifully crinkled edges. Laura bit off one little crinkle and it was sweet. "It's maple sugar," said Pa.

Supper was ready, and Laura and Mary laid their little maple sugar cakes by their plates, while they ate the maple syrup on their bread.

After supper Pa took them on his knees as he sat by the fire and told them about his day at Grandpa's and the sugar snow.

"All winter," Pa said, "Grandpa has been making wooden buckets for the maple syrup. When the first warm weather came, he took the buckets out into the woods and put each one by a maple tree. Then he drilled a small hole in the tree so that the sap could run out."

"After all the buckets were full, he boiled all the sap in a big iron kettle until it turned into maple syrup. Then he cooled some of that sweet syrup into cakes of hard, brown maple sugar."

"Is that why it's called a sugar snow, because Grandpa made sugar?" asked Laura.

"No," said Pa. "It's called a sugar snow because a snow at this time of year helps the trees to make more sap for the syrup."

Then it was time for bed. By the time Laura and
Mary had washed their sticky fingers and were snug
in their beds, Pa and his fiddle were both singing
them off to sleep.